MR.MEN

Favourite Tales

DEAN

This book belongs to

....

EGMONT
We bring stories to life

www.ilovemrmen.co.uk

Printed and published under licence from
Price Stern Sloan, Inc., Los Angeles.
Original creation by Roger Hargreaves
Illustrated by Adam Hargreaves

This edition published in Great Britain in 2011 by Dean,
an imprint of Egmont UK Limited,
239 Kensington High Street, London W8 6SA

Printed and bound in Singapore
ISBN 978 0 6035 6337 9

3 5 7 9 10 8 6 4 2

Contents

MR. MESSY

messing about in the snow

BATH

Mr Messy is the messiest person you are ever likely to meet.

He never has a bath.

His bathtub is full of cobwebs.

And his windows are so dirty he can't see out of them.

Which is why it was two days before he realised that it had snowed.

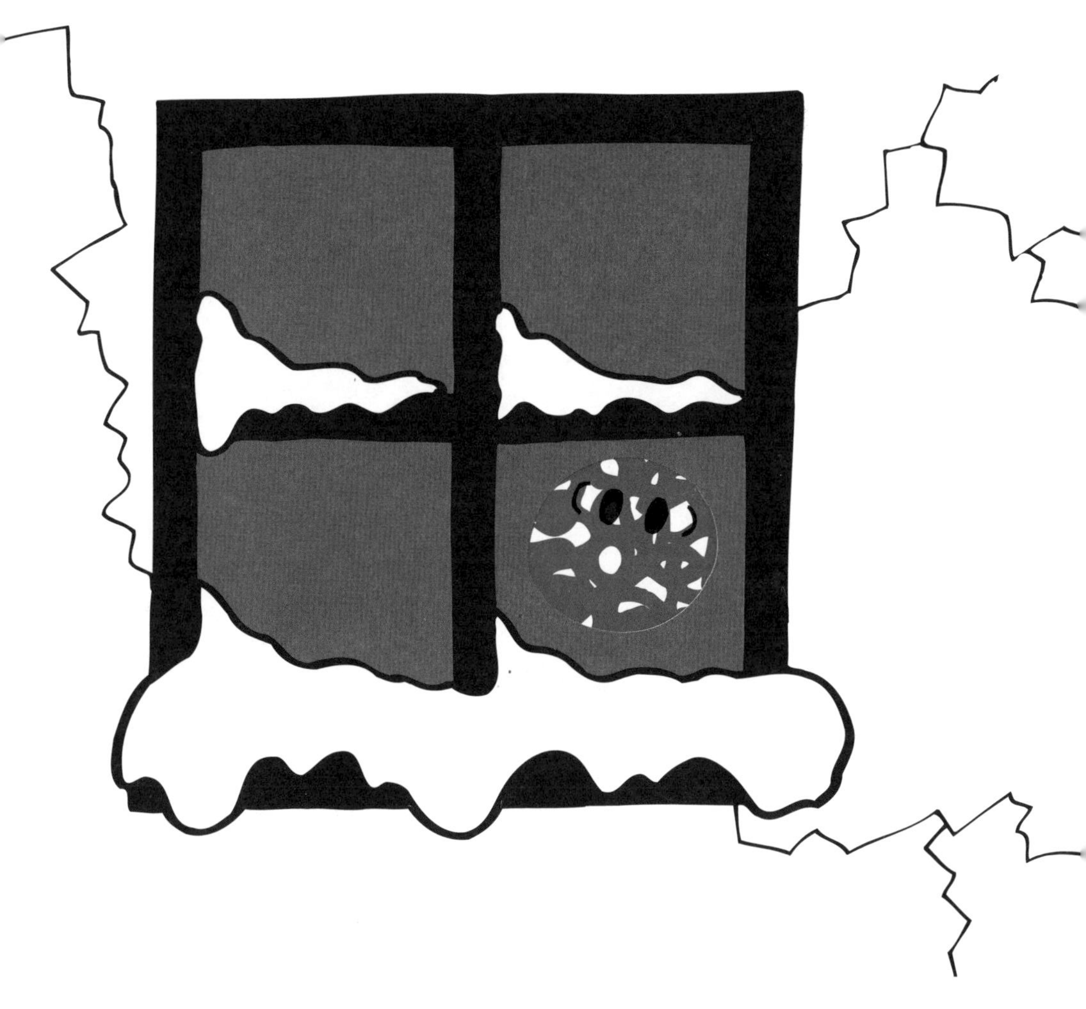

Mr Messy's garden is normally the messiest in the street.

Unlike the garden next door.

But now, with a covering of snow, you couldn't tell them apart.

Mr Messy went outside and promptly tripped over a rake hidden under the snow.

A rake that had been lying there for three years!

Mr Messy walked down to the shed at the bottom of his garden.

A shed so full of odds and ends and bits and bobs that the door would not shut.

Mr Messy knew that underneath all that rubbish there was a toboggan.

So he pulled out all the odds and ends and bits and bobs, until eventually he found his toboggan at the back of the shed.

And then do you think Mr Messy put everything back in the shed?

Don't be silly!

Messy old Mr Messy.

Mr Messy spent the rest of the day playing in the snow.

He tobogganed, and he threw snowballs, and he made snowmen.

He had the best, and busiest, day that he could remember for a long time.

But there was one thing that made it even better.

Something that he enjoyed best of all.

Being messy!

You see, Mr Messy is so grubby that whatever he touches he makes as grubby and as messy as he is.

Everywhere he went he left messy footprints.

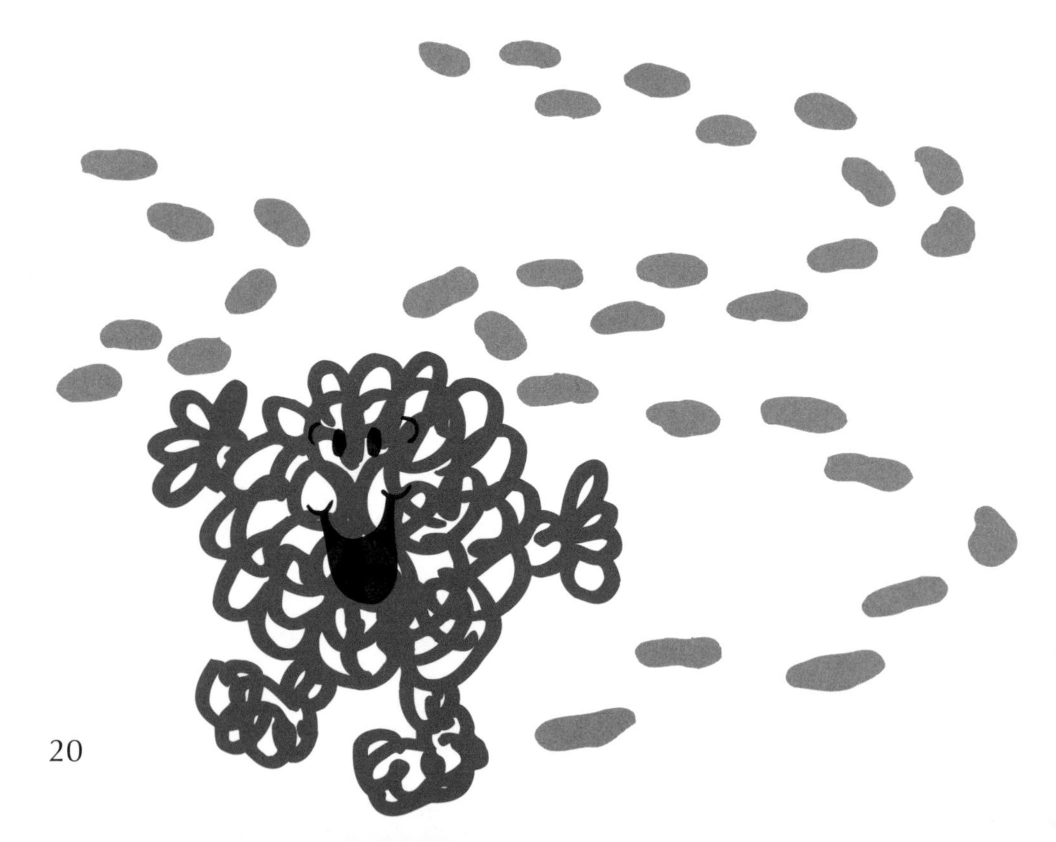

And messy toboggan marks.

And messy snowballs.

And even messy snowmen.

By the end of the day Mr Messy's garden was once again the messiest in the street.

Mr Messy went indoors a happy man, and wiped his feet ... on the carpet!

loses his memory

Mr Bump is the sort of person who is always having accidents.

Small accidents.

Medium-sized accidents.

And big accidents.
Lots and lots of accidents.

One day Mr Bump got out of bed, or rather, he fell out of bed as he did every morning.

He drew back the curtains and opened the window.

It was a beautiful day.

He leant on the window sill and breathed in deeply and ... fell out of the window.

BUMP!

Mr Bump sat up and rubbed his head.
And as he rubbed, it dawned on him that he had no idea where he was.

He had no idea whose garden he was sitting in.

He had no idea whose house he was sitting in front of.

And he had no idea who he was.

Mr Bump had lost his memory.

Mr Bump walked up to his garden gate and looked down the lane.

Mr Muddle was passing by.

"Good afternoon," said Mr Muddle.

As you and I know, it was morning.
But Mr Muddle, not surprisingly, always gets things in a muddle.

"I seem to have lost my memory," said Mr Bump. "Do you know what my name is?"

"You're Mr Careful," said Mr Muddle.

"Thank you," said Mr Bump.

Mr Bump went into town.

The first person he met was Mrs Packet the grocer, carrying an armful of groceries.

"Hello," said Mr Bump, "I'm Mr Careful, can I help?"

"Just the person! I need someone careful to deliver these eggs."

Mr Bump took the eggs from Mrs Packet and set off down the high street.

And because he was Mr Bump he slipped and fell on the eggs, breaking all of them.

"You're not all that careful, are you?" said Mrs Packet.

"Sorry," said Mr Bump.

He walked on past the dairy. Mr Bottle the manager came out.

"I'm looking for someone to drive the milk float," he said. "What's your name?"

"Mr Careful," replied Mr Bump.

"Perfect," said Mr Bottle. "I need someone careful to do the milk round."

Mr Bump set off down the road.

As he rounded the corner he hit the curb and the milk float turned over, smashing all the milk bottles.

"Well, that wasn't very carefully done, was it?" said Mr Bottle.

"Sorry," said Mr Bump.

Then he met Mr Brush the painter, who was up a ladder, painting.

"Hello," said Mr Bump. "I'm Mr Careful. Do you need a hand?"

"Yes please," replied Mr Brush. "I need someone careful to pass me that paint pot."

Mr Bump began to climb the ladder.

And being Mr Bump he fell off and the pot of paint landed on his head.

Mr Bump went for a walk.
"I don't understand it," he said to himself.

"My name is Mr Careful, but I can't do anything carefully!"

It was then that he walked into a tree.

BUMP!

And bumped his head.

An apple fell out of the tree into his hand.
"That's odd," he said to himself.
"How did I get here? The last thing I remember is opening my bedroom window."

" ... And where did all this paint come from?"

You know, don't you?

Just at that moment Farmer Fields turned up.

"Careful ... " he called.

"That sounds familiar," said Mr Bump, and fell down the bank into the river.

MR. TICKLE

in a tangle

Now, who does that extraordinarily long arm belong to?

Of course! Mr Tickle.

And Mr Tickle's long, long arms come in very handy.

They can reach kites caught in trees.

They can answer the phone when Mr Tickle is in the bath.

But, most importantly, they are splendidly perfect for tickling!

Tickling people around corners.

Tickling people through upstairs windows.

And even tickling people on the other side of letter boxes!

However, there are days when those extraordinarily long arms are not so handy.

Days when they are nothing but a nuisance.

Days like last Monday.

Mr Tickle was lying in bed eating breakfast when he heard his garden gate open.

It was Mr Stamp, the postman.

Quick as a flash Mr Tickle sent one of his long arms down the stairs to tickle Mr Stamp.

Or, that is what he intended to do, but somehow or other, his arm got tangled up in the banisters.

Poor Mr Tickle!

It took him an hour to untangle his arm!

The letter Mr Stamp had delivered was an invitation from Mr Uppity, for lunch at the Grand Hotel.

Mr Tickle took the bus to town and sat on the upper deck.

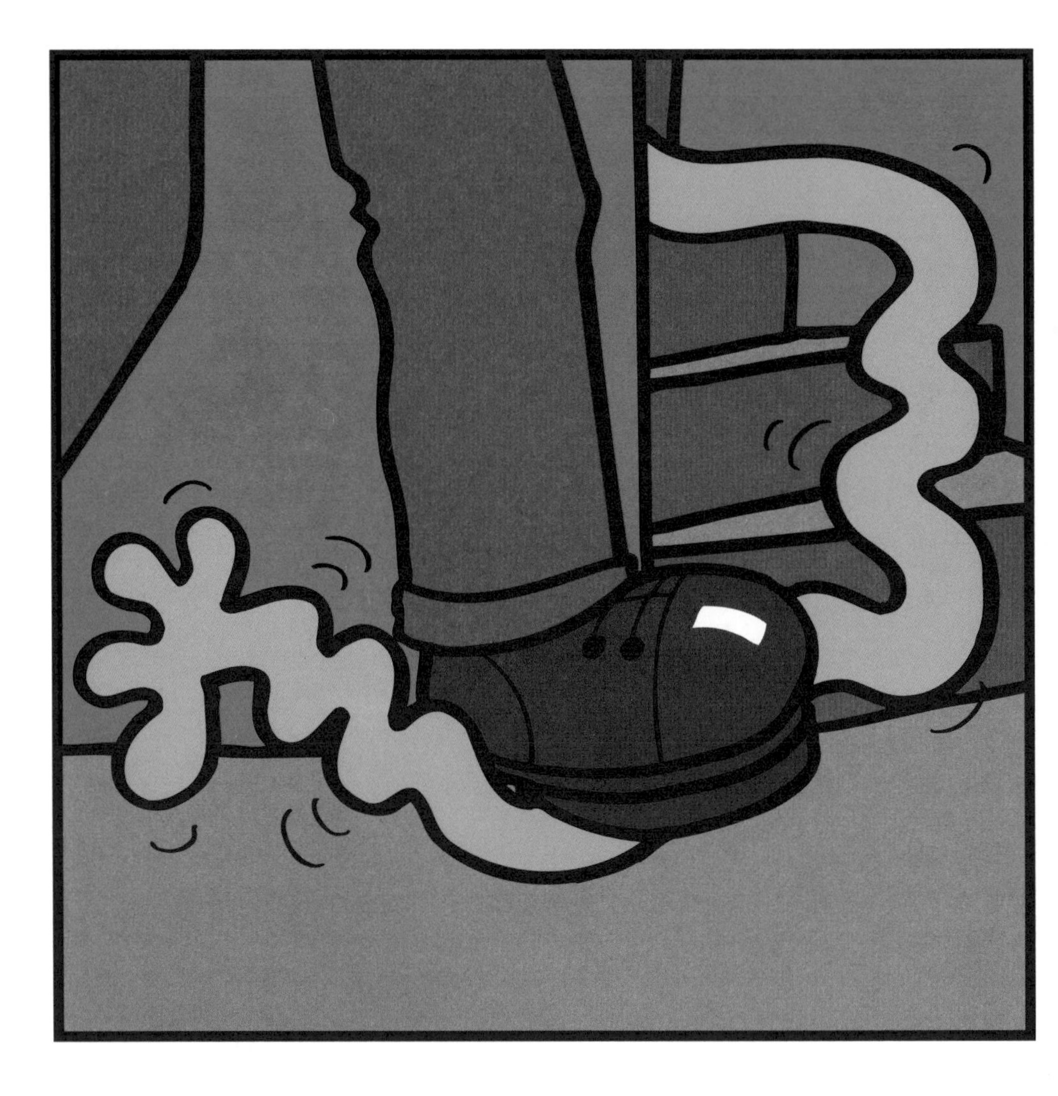

Mr Tickle sent one of his long arms down the stairs to tickle the bus driver, but, somehow or other, the ticket inspector trod on his arm!

OUCH!

Mr Tickle arrived at the Grand Hotel and rushed through the revolving door.

Or rather he tried to, but, somehow or other, his arms caught in the door.

The fire brigade had to be called out to untangle his arms, by which time he had missed lunch.

Poor Mr Tickle.

No lunch, and even worse,
no tickles!

It was a very sad Mr Tickle who set off for home.

Suddenly he heard something.

He stopped. Somebody was approaching from around the corner.

Mr Tickle smiled to himself.

And sent both his arms around the corner to tickle that somebody.

But that somebody was Little Miss Naughty.

And she tied those extraordinarily long arms together in a knot!

When he got home, Mr Tickle fell back into his armchair.

What a terrible day.

Not one tickle!

Suddenly there was a knock at the door.

It was Little Miss Tiny.

Mr Tickle stretched out one of his extraordinarily long arms.

Well, one tickle was better than none.
Even if it was only a tiny tickle!

MR. HAPPY
finds a hobby

Mr Happy is a happy sort of fellow. He lives in Happyland, which is a happy sort of place.

Behind his house there is a wood full of happy birds and on the other side of the wood there is a lake full of happy fish.

Now, one day, not that long ago, Mr Happy went for a walk down through the wood.

As he came to the shore of the lake he heard an unusual sound.

A sound that is seldom heard in Happyland.

It was the sound of somebody moaning and grumbling.

Mr Happy peered round the trunk of a tree.

At the edge of the lake there was somebody fishing.

Fishing and grumbling.

And grumbling and fishing.

It was Mr Grumble.

"Good morning, Mr Grumble," said Mr Happy.

"Ssssh!" ssshed Mr Grumble.

"Sorry," whispered Mr Happy. "Have you caught anything?"

"Yes! I've caught a cold!" grumbled Mr Grumble.

"I've been sitting here all night. I hate fishing!"

"Then, why *are* you fishing?" asked Mr Happy.

"Because Mr Quiet said it was fun! And, you see I'm trying to find something I enjoy doing. Something I can do as a hobby."

"Hmmm," pondered Mr Happy. "I might be able to help. Come on, let's see if we can find you a hobby."

As they walked along, Mr Happy thought, long and hard and as he thought Mr Grumble grumbled.

He grumbled about the noise the birds were making.

He grumbled about having to walk.

But most of all he grumbled about not having a hobby.

Grumble, grumble, grumble.

First of all they met Mr Rush in his car. Mr Happy explained what they were doing.

"What's your hobby?" asked Mr Grumble.

"Speed!" said Mr Rush. "Hop in!"

And they did. Mr Grumble very quickly decided that he did not like going fast.

Next they met Little Miss Giggles.

"What's your hobby?" asked Mr Grumble.

"I ... tee hee ... like ... tee hee ... giggling," giggled Miss Giggles.

So they went to the circus to see the clowns.

Little Miss Giggles giggled, Mr Happy laughed and Mr Grumble ... frowned!

"I hate custard pies," grumbled Mr Grumble.

It proved to be a very long day for Mr Happy.
They went everywhere.
They went to Little Miss Splendid's house.
But Mr Grumble did not like hats.

They went to Mr Mischief's house.

But Mr Grumble did not like practical jokes.

They bounced with Mr Bounce.

And they looked through keyholes with Mr Nosey.

But nothing was right. In fact, nothing was left.

Mr Happy had run out of ideas.

As the sun was setting, they saw Mr Impossible coming towards them down the lane.

"Now, if anybody can help us that somebody ought to be Mr Impossible," said Mr Happy.

"Hello," he said. "You're good at the impossible. Can you think of a hobby that Mr Grumble would enjoy?"

"That ..." said Mr Impossible.

"Yes ..." said Mr Happy and Mr Grumble together.

"... would be impossible," said Mr Impossible.

"Grrr!" growled Mr Grumble, and stomped off home.

It was whilst drinking a cup of tea the next morning that Mr Happy had an idea.

A perfectly obvious idea.

He rushed round to Mr Grumble's house.

"I've got it!" cried Mr Happy. "You can take up fishing."

"Fishing!? But I hate fishing."

"I know, but what do you do while you are fishing?" asked Mr Happy.

"I don't know."

"You grumble," said Mr Happy. "And what do you like doing most of all?"

"I like ..." and then it dawned on Mr Grumble. "I like grumbling!"

Mr Grumble looked at Mr Happy and then for the first time in a very long time he smiled.

A very small smile, but a smile all the same.

MR. SMALL

a big day out

Mr Small was out for a walk.

He was feeling more than a little sorry for himself.

It wasn't much fun being as small as he was.

He sat down under a tree and closed his eyes.

"I do so wish I was bigger," he sighed.

"Much, much bigger," he added.

Now, Mr Small did not know that there was a wizard lying down on the other side of the tree.

He had stopped for a snooze and, just as he had been dozing off, the wizard had overheard Mr Small's wish.

The wizard smiled to himself.

Without even opening his eyes, he muttered some magic words under his breath and then went back to sleep.

As Mr Small lay there, something really quite remarkable happened.

Something really quite remarkably magic.

Mr Small began to grow.

And grow.

And grow.

Until he bumped his head on a branch!

When he crawled out from underneath the tree and stood up he was taller than the tree.

Much taller.

"Gosh," said Mr Small.

He could not believe his eyes.

He could not believe his size!

He went for a walk to try out his new size.

It was wonderful.

He could see over the top of everything.

He leap-frogged over trees and jumped over rivers.

He gave Mr Uppity the shock of his life.

He was stronger than Mr Strong.

Noisier than Mr Noisy.

And taller than Mr Tall!

He could even make his fingers meet when he put his arms around Mr Greedy's tummy!

Mr Small had a marvellous day, and as the sun set he lay down in a field and went to sleep.

As Mr Small slept he shrank back to his normal size.

For you see, the wizard had cast a spell that would only last one day.

When Mr Small woke up it was dark.

"What a wonderful dream," he said to himself, and got up to walk home.

But he found he couldn't. He was surrounded by a wall!

However, when he felt along the bottom, he discovered that he could lift up the wall.

It was light outside, and when he crawled out Mr Small could not believe his eyes.

He had been trapped underneath a hat!

A hat that looked just like his own, but it was much, much bigger.

"Well, I never," said Mr Small. "Maybe it wasn't a dream after all."

That sleepy old wizard had forgotten to finish off his spell properly.

He had forgotten to make sure Mr Small's hat would shrink back to the right size.

Mr Small now had a ten-gallon hat.

A ten-gallon hat for a pint-sized person!

NEWS